ISBN 978-0-545-66349-6

Text copyright © 2011 by Jean Reidy. Illustrations copyright © 2011 by Margaret Chodos-Irvine.
All rights reserved. Published by Scholastic Inc., 557 Broadway, New York, NY 10012,
by arrangement with Hyperion Books for Children, an imprint of Disney Book Group, LLC.
SCHOLASTIC and associated logos are trademarks and/or registered trademarks of Scholastic Inc.

12 11 10 9 8 7 6 5 4 3 2 1   14 15 16 17 18 19/0

Printed in the U.S.A.   40

First Scholastic printing, February 2014

This book is set in Bernhard Gothic.
Designed by Judythe Sieck

Light Up the Night

By Jean Reidy

Pictures by Margaret Chodos-Irvine

SCHOLASTIC INC.

This is me.

This

is my

universe.

These are my galaxy stars so bright—
they light up the heavens late at night

in my own little piece of the universe.

These are the planets that circle the sun,
which hides its face when the day is done,

while stars glow bright
and light up the night,

in my own little piece of the universe.

This is my planet, the one we call Earth,

N|

|S

with poles at its ends and equator its girth.

It's one of the planets that circle the sun,
which hides its face when the day is done,
while stars glow bright
and light up the night,

in my own little piece of the universe.

This is my hemisphere, half the ball,
with ice caps and islands and mountains tall.

It's half the Earth,
which circles the sun,
which hides its face when the day is done,
while stars glow bright
and light up the night,

in my own little piece of the universe.

This is my continent, far and wide.
It kisses an ocean on either side,

on half the Earth,
which circles the sun,
which hides its face when the day is done,
while stars glow bright
and light up the night,

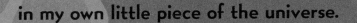

in my own little piece of the universe.

This is my country, with highlands and plains,
with farmlands and cities and highways and trains.

It sits on my continent, far and wide,
which kisses an ocean on either side,
on half the Earth,
which circles the sun,
which hides its face when the day is done,
    while stars glow bright
    and light up the night,

in my own little piece of the universe.

This is my town, and this is my street,

with friends I know and new ones to meet.
It's part of my country, with highlands and plains,
with farmlands and cities and highways and trains.
It sits on my continent, far and wide,
which kisses an ocean on either side,
on half the Earth,
which circles the sun,
which hides its face when the day is done,
while stars glow bright
and light up the night,

in my own little piece of the universe.

This is my house—the one in between,
with shutters, a porch, and a door painted green.

It's built in my town,
right here on my street,
with friends I know and new ones to meet.
All part of my country, with highlands and plains,
with farmlands and cities and highways and trains.
It sits on my continent, far and wide,
which kisses an ocean on either side,
on half the Earth,
which circles the sun,
which hides its face when the day is done,

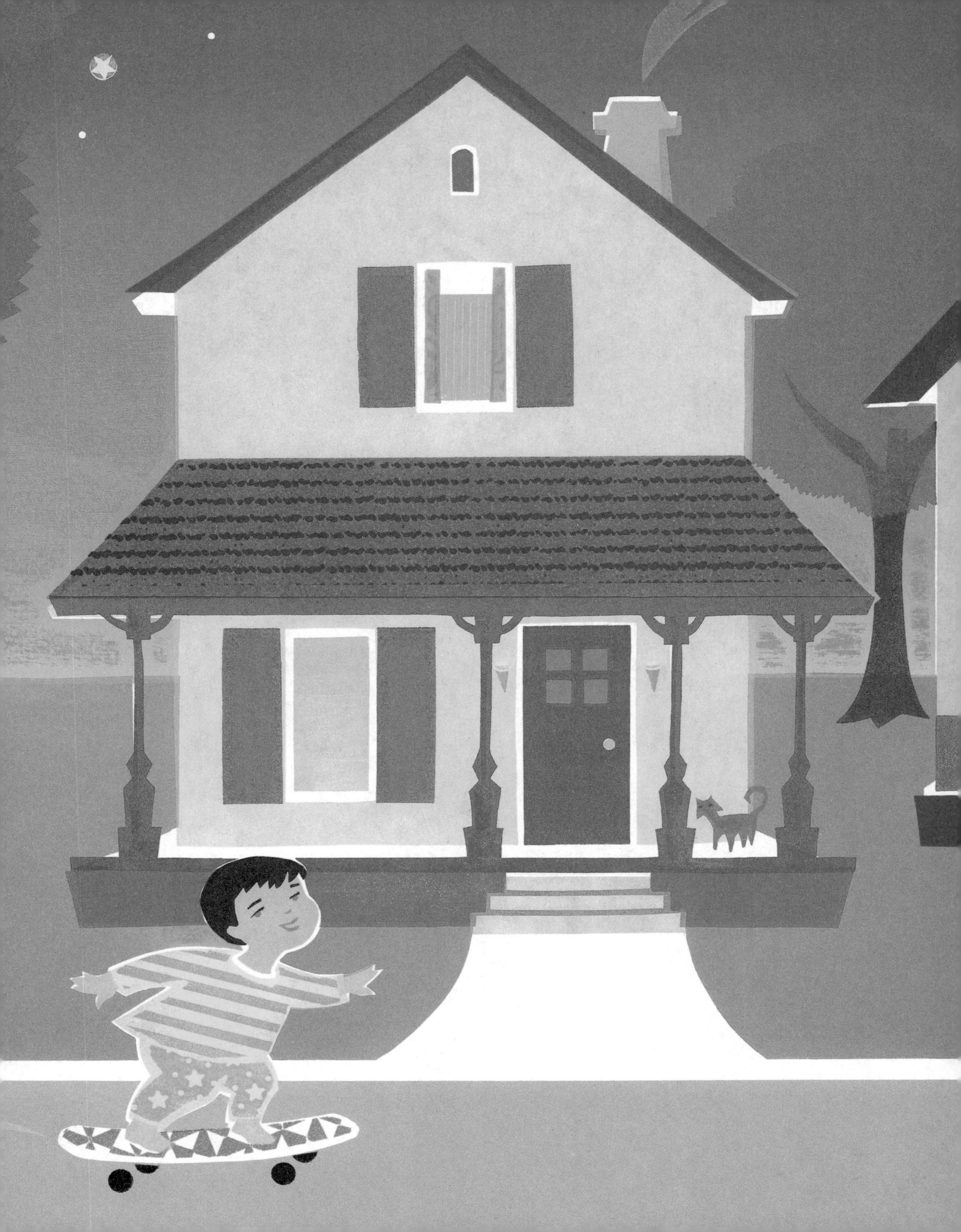

while stars glow bright
and light up the night,

in my own little piece of the universe.

This is my room, with my name on the door,

and my dinosaur lamp, and my rug on the floor.

Right here in my house, the one in between,
with shutters, a porch, and a door painted green.
It's built in my town,
right here on my street,
with friends I know and new ones to meet.
All part of my country, with highlands and plains,
with farmlands and cities and highways and trains.
It sits on my continent, far and wide,
which kisses an ocean on either side,
on half the Earth,
which circles the sun,
which hides its face when the day is done,
while stars glow bright
and light up the night,

in my own little piece of the universe.

This is me, in my cozy bed,

under my blanket, white and red,

right here in my room,

inside my house,

on my street,

in my town,

part of my country,

here on my continent,

on half the Earth,

circling the sun,

while stars glow bright
and light up the night . . .

in my own little piece of the universe.

To Mom —JR

For Judythe, the best in the universe. —MC-1